Making Their Mark: Women in Sports™

Monica Seles
Champion Tennis Player

Liza N. Burby

The Rosen Publishing Group's
PowerKids Press™
New York

Published in 1997 by The Rosen Publishing Group, Inc.
29 East 21st Street, New York, NY 10010

Copyright © 1997 by The Rosen Publishing Group, Inc.

All rights reserved. No part of this book may be reproduced in any form without permission in writing from the publisher, except by a reviewer.

First Edition

Book Design: Erin McKenna

Photo Credits: Cover and pp. 7, 11, 15, 16 © AP/Wide World Photos, Inc.; p. 4 © REUTERS/Darrin Braybrook/Archive Photos; p. 8 © REUTERS/Ray Stubblebine/Archive Photos; p. 12 © REUTERS/Gary Cameron/Archive Photos; p. 19 © AP Photos/Malcolm Clarke; p. 20 © REUTERS/Michael Lackel/Archive Photos.

Burby, Liza N.
    Monica Seles / by Liza N. Burby
        p.   cm. — (Making their mark)
    Includes index.
    Summary: Follows the life of the tennis star who became the youngest winner of a Grand Slam title in over 100 years, from her childhood in Yugoslavia through her traumatic attack during a match in Germany in 1993 to her comeback in 1995.
    ISBN 0-8239-5068-9 (library bound)
    1. Seles, Monica—Juvenile literature. 2. Tennis players—Yugoslavia—Biography—Juvenile literature. [1. Seles, Monica, 1973- . 2. Tennis players. 3. Women—Biography.] I. Title. II. Series: Burby, Liza N. Making their mark.
GV994.S45B87 1997
796.342'092—dc21
    [B]
                                                                           96–30002
                                                                           CIP
                                                                            AC

Manufactured in the United States of America

Contents

1	Monica Tries Tennis	5
2	A Powerful Hitter	6
3	Sportswoman of the Year	9
4	A Strong Young Player	10
5	A Young Professional	13
6	French Open Champion	14
7	A Noisy Player	17
8	A Terrible Day	18
9	Strong Enough to Play Again	21
10	Monica Is Still Number One	22
	Glossary	23
	Index	24

Monica Tries Tennis

Monica Seles was born on December 2, 1973, in Novi Sad, Yugoslavia. It's hard to believe now, but when Monica was little, she didn't like tennis. She was six years old when her father first taught her to play tennis. But Monica didn't have much fun learning the sport, so she decided to stop playing. Then her older brother, Zoltan, won a **trophy** (TRO-fee) at the Yugoslav Junior Tennis **Championships** (CHAM-pee-un-ships). Monica thought she might like to try to win a trophy too.

◀ When Monica's brother started to win tournaments, Monica became interested in tennis.

A Powerful Hitter

Monica's father was more than her tennis teacher. He was also a cartoonist and filmmaker. To help Monica learn the sport, he made cartoon movies about how to play tennis. He also drew funny cartoons on the tennis balls she used. Most tennis players are right-handed. Because Monica is left-handed, her father taught her to hold the tennis racket with two hands for both her **forehand** (FOR-hand) and **backhand** (BAK-hand) **strokes** (STROHKS). This made her a very powerful hitter.

Monica is one of the only left-handed players to have a double-handed grip. ▶

Sportswoman of the Year

It didn't take long for Monica to be a top junior player. She won her first **tournament** (TERN-uh-ment) when she was eight years old. She won first place at the European Championships two years in a row. She became the youngest player ever to be named Yugoslavia's Sportswoman of the Year. Then in 1985, she played at a tournament in Florida. A famous tennis teacher named Nick Bollettieri asked her to come to his tennis camp with other top junior players.

◀ Monica started winning tournaments at a very young age.

A Strong Young Player

In 1986, when Monica was thirteen, the Seles family left Yugoslavia and moved to Florida. Monica began to train with Nick. She was a strong player. Monica hit the ball so well that Nick had trouble finding girls who would practice with her. Even some of the boys walked off the court when she played against them.

Monica could beat anybody on the court. She did well off the court too. Monica studied hard and got very good grades in school.

Monica trained every day to improve her tennis skills. ▶

A Young Professional

Monica began playing in **professional** (pro-FESH-uh-nul) women's events when she was fourteen. At first she didn't win. But in 1989, she surprised tennis fans when she beat one of the top players, Chris Evert, in the Virginia Slims Tournament. She went on to the French Open, where she played Steffi Graf, the number one player in the world, for the first time. She lost the tournament. But Monica would have many other chances to beat Steffi. At the end of that year, Monica was the sixth best women's player in the world.

◀ By the end of her first year in professional tennis, Monica was one of the top ten women players in the world.

French Open Champion

In 1990, Monica grew six inches. She had to get used to playing as a much taller player. Monica said that the net seemed lower and the racket seemed lighter. She lost her first few tournaments that year. But soon she got used to her new height. She worked her way up to being the third best player in the world.

That year, at the German Open, she beat Steffi Graf for the first time. Then she beat Steffi again at the French Open. Monica became the youngest French Open champion ever.

Monica continued to win awards for her tennis playing. Here she is seen with tennis player Stefan Edberg at an awards ceremony. ▶

A Noisy Player

By 1991, Monica was the top women's player in the world. Not only was she known as a powerful player, but she was also known for being noisy. Whenever Monica hit the ball, she grunted loudly. Once, she got in trouble during a match for grunting as she played. But when she tried to stop, she lost the game. When she started grunting again during her matches, she started winning tournaments again. Monica still grunts during her matches.

◄ Monica says she doesn't even realize she's grunting when she plays.

A Terrible Day

Monica and Steffi continued to meet in tournament **finals** (FY-nulz). Sometimes Monica would win. Sometimes Steffi would win. In 1993, Monica and Steffi were playing in a tournament in Germany, Steffi's home country. One of Steffi's fans did something terrible to Monica. He stabbed her in the back with a knife during a break between games. The fan said he did it because he wanted Steffi to win. Monica's back healed quickly, but she was scared to play tennis again.

After Monica's accident, she just watched tennis matches instead of playing. ▶

Strong Enough to Play Again

Monica took a break from tennis for about two years. During that time she grew another inch, to five feet, ten-and-a-half inches. She also became a **citizen** (SIT-ih-zen) of the United States. Monica kept training by running and playing tennis with friends. But she had a lot of nightmares about what happened to her during the tournament in Germany. Her father told her to speak with a **psychologist** (sy-KOL-uh-jist). By talking to the psychologist about her fears, Monica soon felt strong enough to play professional tennis again.

◀ Talking out her fears about playing tennis again helped Monica to get back on the court.

Monica Is Still Number One

Monica returned to women's tennis in 1995. Her fans and her tennis-playing friends were glad to see her. They said that women's tennis was not as interesting without powerful, noisy Monica playing. Even though she was away from tennis for two years, Monica is still a champion. She has won many tournaments. She even played on the U.S. team at the 1996 Olympic Games in Atlanta, Georgia. Today, Monica still battles for the top spot with her old **rival** (RY-vul) Steffi Graf.

Glossary

backhand (BAK-hand) A way to hold and swing a tennis racket so that the back of the hand holding the racket faces out.

championship (CHAM-pee-un-ship) A game to see who is the best player.

citizen (SIT-ih-zen) A person who is born in or chooses to live in a certain country.

finals (FY-nulz) The last in a series of tournament games.

forehand (FOR-hand) A way to hold and swing a tennis racket so that the front of the hand holding the racket faces out.

professional (pro-FESH-uh-nul) A person who gets paid to play a sport.

psychologist (sy-KOL-uh-jist) A person who helps people work out their problems by talking with them.

rival (RY-vul) Someone who tries to beat someone else at something.

stroke (STROHK) The swing a tennis player makes to hit a ball.

tournament (TERN-uh-ment) An event in which many games are played to see who is the best player.

trophy (TRO-fee) A statue or cup given to the winner of a game.

Index

B
backhand, 6
Bollettieri, Nick, 9, 10

C
championships, 5, 9
citizen, 21

E
Evert, Chris, 13

F
fans, 18, 22
finals, 18
forehand, 6

F
French Open, 13, 14

G
German Open, 14
Graf, Steffi, 13, 14, 18, 22
grunting, 17

L
left-handed, 6

M
matches, 17

O
Olympic Games, 22

P
psychologist, 21

R
rival, 22

S
stabbing, 18
strokes, 6

T
tournaments, 9, 13, 14, 17, 18, 19, 21, 22
training, 10, 21
trophy, 5